THE DAY THAT
ALIENS
nearly
Ate Our
BRAINS

THE DAY THAT ALIENS nearly Ate Our BRAINS

TOM MCLAUGHLIN

WALKER
BOOKS

First published in Great Britain 2018 by Walker Books Ltd
87 Vauxhall Walk, London SE11 5HJ

2 4 6 8 10 9 7 5 3 1

Text and illustrations © 2018 Tom McLaughlin
Cover design © 2018 Walker Books Ltd

This book has been typeset in Stempel Schneidler

Printed and bound in Great Britain by CPI Group (UK) Ltd

British Library Cataloguing in Publication Data:
a catalogue record for this book is available from the British Library

ISBN 978-1-4063-7579-4

www.walker.co.uk

recipe is for informational and/or entertainment purposes only;
please check ingredients carefully if you have any allergies and,
if in doubt, consult a health professional.

To my excellent coffee provider
and amazing wife, Elle x

"An inch to the left ... now an inch to the right ... that's it, almost there! That's it! One small step for man, one giant leap forward in sneakily watching

using next door's TV feed!" Freddy yelled in delight.

"Finally, we can watch the title clash between Bone Crusher Bill and Bloodthirsty Derek."

"Well *yooou* can. *I* can't see a thing from up here." There, standing on a chair, holding a silver cone and wearing a colander on his head, wobbled Freddy's best friend Sal.

"I told you, someone has to point the satellite dish at next door's transmitter; it's the only way to watch the big fight. You lost at paper, scissors, stone so stop complaining."

"It's not a satellite dish, it's the cone your dog had to wear round his head when he had his bits taken off, covered in tin foil," Sal protested.

Both Freddy and Sal looked over at the

dog, who sighed a sad sigh and went back to sleep.

"Relax, you do the first hour, I'll do the second."

"I HAVE TO STAND LIKE THIS FOR A WHOLE **HOUR?!**"

Sal shouted. "I can't feel my left buttock."

"Well I'm not feeling it for you!" Freddy shuddered.

"No, I mean it has pins and needles in it. It's both horrible and strangely pleasurable at the same time."

"A little more to the left." Freddy waved, squinting at the TV as it fizzed in and out of signal.

"I don't think that's a good idea..." Sal whimpered.

"Why?" Freddy asked, staring at the screen.

THUMP!

The whole room shook as Sal landed in a heap on the ground and the colander rolled to Freddy's feet.

"That's why," Sal said, rubbing his head.

"Oopsy," Freddy sighed. "How many fingers am I holding up?"

Sal squinted. "Which of your four hands am I supposed to be looking at?"

"Hmm, maybe have a sit down," Freddy said sympathetically. "It was a terrible idea anyway."

This was not the first hair-brained scheme that Freddy and Sal had attempted. There was the time they tried to invent hover-sock. The scorch marks were still visible on the ceiling of Freddy's bedroom. There was also the occasion Freddy and Sal rewired the washing machine to turn it into a giant candyfloss machine, and Freddy's dad's pants came out fluorescent pink. But that's what being eleven was all about, getting into scrapes and turning your best friend into a human satellite dish.

"Well I guess we can't watch the wrestling ... I'm sooooo bored. What now?" Freddy puffed.

"You know what we could do..." Sal said quietly.

"No!" Freddy snapped. "Don't say it."

"We could see if we can get the goldfish to speak again?" Sal said casually.

"I can't believe you said it ... for the last time, Sal, fish can't talk!"

"You weren't there, you didn't hear him!"

"NOBODY HEARD HIM. HE'S. A. FISH!!!"

It had been a few weeks previously, on another boring afternoon, when Sal had attempted to hypnotize Freddy's fish, Perkins, with the belief that they could convince him to talk. Freddy had been downstairs fetching a snack for the pair of them, when Sal claimed he'd heard Perkins say the word "banana".

"Well I can't think of anything else to do," Sal said, sitting on the end of the bed and looking up at the ceiling. Freddy's

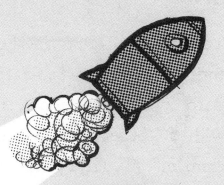

bedroom was an Aladdin's cave of gizmos and gadgets, posters of planets and space rockets. Freddy was a bit of a dreamer. Sal and he were always being accused of having their heads in the clouds, *but what's wrong with that?* Freddy thought. *At least things are interesting up in the stars, not like down here on planet Earth.* Their tiny town of beige houses seemed to suck the life out of everything and everyone.

Just then a head popped round the door. It was Freddy's mum.

"Did I hear a thud?" she asked, eyeing the pair of them suspiciously.

"Err, no Mum."

"Are you sure?" she said as she looked at the TV hissing in and out of signal.

"That's a lovely hair-do you've got there. Is it new?" Sal interrupted.

"Oh why yes, Sal. How thoughtful of you to notice." Freddy's mum smiled.

"I might get one of those myself." Sal grinned.

"I'm not sure platinum-blonde tinted highlights would suit you, Sal. But thank you. Anyway, I only came up to tell you that me and your dad are off to the garden centre. We'll be back later. You two all right on your own?"

"Yes Mum." Freddy nodded. With that, she shut the door and bounced down the stairs.

"That was close." Freddy sighed.

"The old 'that's a nice hair-do' trick, works every time."

"Oh I can't take it any more! This place is so dull," Freddy said, staring out on to the street, "nothing exciting ever happens here."

"Aren't you forgetting about the time Wolverhampton was hit with that terrible storm?"

"Oh, the great drizzle of '83? Don't, my nan still talks about that. Can you turn the TV off? It keeps buzzing at me."

Sal looked at the TV as it crackled and whizzed into life. "Must be picking up a signal from next door still."

"GREETINGS EARTHLINGS!"

Freddy looked at Sal. "What?"

"What? I thought you said that?"

"GREETINGS EARTHLINGS I SAID. PLEASE BE HOW I EXPECT YOU RESPOND AND DO THE REPLYING BACK NOW."

came the strangely worded reply, as if it was English but not English.

Freddy and Sal looked at each other.

"Oh. My. Crikey! It's Perkins! He's trying to communicate with us Freddy!" Sal ran up and put his head next to the fish bowl.

"HELLO PERKINS, I AM SAL, TALK TO ME YOU FISHY GENIUS."

"Er, Sal..." Freddy whispered.

"TELL ME, WHAT'S IT LIKE TO BE UNDERWATER? HOW DO YOU SNEEZE? DO YOU LIKE SWIMMING IN YOUR OWN WEE-WEE?" Sal cried, shouting at the fish as if it were an exchange student.

"Sal…" Freddy said a little louder.

"TELL ME, DOES BEING WET EVER GET BORING?"

"SAL!" Freddy screamed. "IT'S NOT THE FISH IN THE BOWL TALKING TO US!"

"How do you know?" Sal huffed.

"BECAUSE THERE'S AN ALIEN ON THE TV SCREEN!"

Freddy yelled, pointing at the TV.

"YOUR FRIEND IS RIGHT IN HIS THINKING.
I AM **ALAN** FROM THE PLANET **TWANG** AND
I AM HERE TO DO THE TELLING OF YOU THAT
YOU HAVE UNTIL 10 P.m. TONIGHT UNTIL
THE END OF THE WORLD WHEN I WILL KILL
YOU ALL TO DEATH. TICKETY-TOCK ...

TICKETY-TOCK."

Freddy's finger was trembling, and his mouth was open and a bit dribbly. Sal turned around slowly and stared at the TV. There, on the flickering screen, was a green-headed beast with large bulging eyes and big sticky-out ears. He had an enormous head that rippled and pulsated every time he spoke. He looked exactly like what he was: an alien from another planet.

"What channel is this?" Sal muttered. "Peter Andre's really let himself go."

"It's not a TV show. This is real!"

"YOUR MUCH CLEVERER FRIEND IS VERY RIGHT AT WHAT HE SAYS SMALL EARTH PERSON. I GUESS THAT MEANS HE IS THE SMART HEADED ONE AND YOU ARE THE IDIOT NITWIT WHO VERY MUCH LIKES THE COMPANY OF FISH."

"Eh? I don't like the company of fish. Sometimes, just sometimes, they say things," Sal protested.

"I AM VERY MUCH BORED OF YOU. YOUR FACE SPURTS OUT SILLY MESSAGES."

The alien creature snorted in disgust.

"Wait... What did you say a moment ago?" Freddy interrupted. "You're going to destroy the earth, tonight?"

"YOUR TV SIGNALS HAVE BEEN DRIFTING THROUGH THE GALAXY, WE HAVE WATCHED ALL THE **DAFTY** THINGS THAT YOU AND YOUR KIND HAVE BEEN GETTING UP TO. WE HAVE VERY OFTEN BEEN OBSERVING HOW YOU TALK FROM THE TELEVISION AND WE ARE NOW FLUENT IN ENGLISH **TALKY-TALK.**"

"Well ... not that fluent," Sal muttered under his breath.

"SHUTTY YOUR FACE FLAP!

WE HAVE ALL VERY MUCH HEARD OF YOUR FAMOUS HUMAN JOKES, AND I TELL THIS FOR NOTHING, FISH BOY, I **DO NOT LIKE IT!**"

Alan the alien screamed, before composing himself again.

"WE DECIDED THAT THE GALAXY IS BETTER OFF WITH HUMANS NOT IN IT, INNIT. BUT WE COULDN'T DO THE PIN-POINTING ON THE MAP OF WHERE YOUR PLANET WAS. UNTIL YOU, THE ONE THEY CALL THE FREDDY, SENT A SIGNAL INTO SPACE. SO THANKING YOU VERY MUCH. WE NOW KNOW WHERE YOU LIVE, SO WE COME AND FIND YOU. THANK YOU, THANK YOU..."

"What?" Freddy protested. "I only wanted to watch the wrestling, not start a space war."

"TOO LATE. NOW WE KNOW WHERE YOU ARE, THE INTERGALACTIC KINGDOM OF ... WOLVERHAMPTON."

Alan said, peering at a map.

"WE WILL COME AND TAKE OVER YOUR PLANET AND LEARN FROM YOUR PEOPLE IN THE TIME-HONOURED TRADITION OF TWANG."

"What's that?" Sal asked rather nervously.

"BY LEARNING FROM YOUR BRAINS — NOT JUST YOUR BRAIN THOUGH, BUT CLEVERERERERER PEOPLE'S BRAINS."

Alan said, looking at Sal.

"Well just ask us. You don't need to fly all the way here, it's just a waste of petrol," Freddy said, doing his best to stop a full-scale alien invasion.

"THERE IS ONLY ONE WAY TO LEARN FROM THE BRAINS."

"What's that?" Sal asked again.

"EATING THEm IN OUR mOUTHS. WE EAT THE BRAINS AnD WE DO THE LEARNING. IT IS THE WAY OF THE TwAnG."

"WHAT?! HAVE YOU NEVER HEARD OF A LIBRARY?"

Sal yelled. Freddy looked at the homemade satellite dish. "No, it was an accident, please don't come and eat our brains."

"I AM VERY MUCH BORED OF YOUR UNTRUTHS, IT IS TIME FOR THE MIGHTY ALAN TO GO AND FLY THE SPACESHIP TOWARDS YOUR HORRIBLE WORLD OF NITWITS AND CLOWNS. COME ON BRIAN, PLEASE GO PUT THE HOT WATER KETTLE ON, FOR IT IS TIME TO DRINK TEA, THE NECTAR OF THE TWANG. ALSO I MIGHT HAVE A CRUMPET TOO. ALAN IS RIGHT IN THE MOOD FOR THE CRUMPET."

Just at that moment another head popped onto the TV screen.

"YES MASTER, DESTROYER OF WORLDS, ALMIGHTY WORRIER AND CRUMPET LOVER."

Brian sighed wearily.

"GOODBYE **HUMANS** ... FOR NOW!"

And with that Alan was gone. Freddy rubbed his eyes. For a few seconds he just stared at Sal.

"Did that happen?" Sal asked.

"Yes. Well I think it did," Freddy said, still unable to comprehend what he'd just seen.

"Your mum and dad are going to be well annoyed when they know you've started a space war with alien brain-munchers. They don't even like it when you help yourself to a KitKat."

"What are we going to do?" Freddy cried, checking his watch.

"WE HAVE UNTIL 10 P.M. TO SAVE THE WORLD!"

"We should tell someone. Isn't that what they always say? Tell a responsible adult, a figure of authority, someone who's not to be messed with."

"Yes!" said Freddy. "YES, YES that's a great idea!"

"I know just the person!" Sal grinned.

☆

"Why are you telling me this? Do I look like an idiot? Now go away, before I hit you with my lollipop!" came the angry response.

Sal ducked just in time as a huge fluorescent yellow blur tried to swat him.

"CHANGE OF PLAN!" Sal yelled. "RUN AWAY, RUN AWAY!"

Sal and Freddy galloped down the road.

"HILDA THE ANGRY LOLLIPOP LADY?!"

Freddy shrieked. "That was your great idea, telling a lollipop lady? She's hardly NASA is she?"

"Who's Nessa?" Sal gasped as they hid round the corner.

"Not Nessa, NASA, the people in

America who send space rockets into ...
well ... space."

"Oh..." Sal nodded.

"WAIT. THAT'S IT, WE SHOULD CALL NASA!"

Freddy yelled in delight.

"Brilliant!" Sal agreed. "But how? I mean they probably don't have a direct number."

"You're right," Freddy said, scratching his head. "It's not going to just fall out of the sky, is it? We need help."

"Oh wait, I could ask my uncle Clive!" Sal piped up. "He's at the police station."

"Oh, why, what's he done?" Freddy asked, looking shocked. He'd been friends with Sal for years – he had no idea that his best friend's uncle was some sort of criminal.

"Nothing!" Sal laughed. "He works there!"

"What?!" Freddy said, the grin disappearing from his face as he came to a juddering halt.

"Yeah, he's a policeman."

Freddy said nothing. Sal screwed up his face, trying to work out why Freddy was suddenly annoyed with him. "Oh ... perhaps we should have gone to see a policeman about the incoming alien invasion *first* rather than a lollipop lady with a history of violence?"

"Yer think?!" Freddy smiled sarcastically. "Anything else I should know about your family Sal? Is your great aunt Batman? Is your pet cat the prime minister? All this could be very useful."

"My cousin's been on TV balloon modelling, but I don't think that's going to help a great deal," Sal said.

"Let's go find your uncle," Freddy said, looking at his watch.

"Oh my goodness me, this is an absolute disaster! Something needs to be done straight away!" There, behind the desk of the local police station, a tall man with an impressive moustache picked up the radio and barked, "CODE RED, WE'VE

GOT A CODE RED! Scramble all units, this is an emergency, everyone report to number fifty-seven Coronation Gardens, there's a cat stuck in a tree. Fire up the squad car too!" This was Desk Sergeant Clive West, also known as Sal's uncle.

He slammed the phone down, just as Freddy and Sal walked in.

"Hey boys, how goes it?"

"Not brilliant, the world's about to end," Freddy replied.

"Tell me about it," Sal's uncle sighed. "It's been mayhem here. Mrs Splat's cat Matt got stuck in the tree again. It's a code red."

"WHAT?!" Sal gasped. "A CODE RED? Did you scramble the squad car? What made it run up there in the first place?"

"Got spooked by a squad car ... oh... Anyway," he smiled and clapped his hands, "life goes on. What can I do for you two chaps?"

"Uncle Clive, this is Freddy. He has something very important to tell you." Sal pushed Freddy in front of his uncle. "Go on, tell him Freddy!"

"Well, Mr West," Freddy began. "We were messing around with the TV and a homemade satellite dish and something odd happened. I know this is going to sound rather strange, but I think we've made contact with an alien race; not only that, they want to destroy the world, oh, and eat our brains. I think that's it." Freddy smiled hopefully. Sergeant West looked at both of them very carefully.

"Now, I'm not pointing any fingers, or blaming anyone, all I want is an honest answer. Have you been on the strong cheese again, Sal? Do you remember that time you had some Stilton and you thought a fifty-foot hamster was chasing you?"

"NO!" Freddy and Sal yelled simultaneously.

"Uncle Clive, it's true," Sal pleaded.

"Okay, let's put the news on," Sergeant West said, turning on the box next to him. "I'm sure if the planet is on the verge of annihilation, it'll be on Midlands Today."

"It won't be!" Freddy sighed.

"There's no news anyway," Sal's uncle muttered, "just some show about a man with a big green head. Weird, it's on every channel. Good crikey, Peter Andre's let himself go."

"What?!" Sal said. "Let me see."

"THAT'S HIM!"

they both shouted, looking at the screen.
"Wha—???" Sal's uncle said.

"GREETING FREDDY, LOVER OF THE **WRESTLING**, EATER OF THE **CHEESE**, AND HIS STRANGE SIDE-KICK PERSON, KNOWN TO ALL AS SAL. AND GOOD HELLO TO LARGE EARTH PERSON WHO I DON'T KNOW YET."

"How did you know we were here?" Freddy asked, looking shocked.

"I TOLD YOU, I HAVE BEEN WATCHING YOU. I KNOW WHERE YOU ARE ALL THE TIME. ALSO I WAS WANTING TO ASK YOU FOR A GOOD FAVOUR MY SOON TO BE DEAD EARTHLING. BEFORE WE KILL YOU TO DEATH, CAN YOU LEAVE THE RECIPE FOR THE FOOD-TYPE YOU CALL PUDDING OF RICE OUT SOMEWHERE? I'm KEEN TO mAKE IT TO HAVE WITH YOUR DELICIOUS BRAINS."

"If you GO AWAY maybe we'll give it to you!" Sal shrieked.

"YOU ARE A SPORTING SPOIL PERSON."

Alan grumbled.

"Wait, wait...!" Sergeant West said, putting his hand up, trying to calm the situation down. "No one's getting 'killed to death'. Now who are you and what do you really want? Enough of this nonsense about being an alien. Tell me who you really are."

"I Am ALAn FRom THE PLAnET TwAnG."

"You're Loopy from the planet Bananas, more like."

"I Am wARRIOR OF mY PEOPLE AnD I'vE COmE TO DESTROY YOUR WORLD, EAT YOUR TInY BRAiNS, YOU PLAnET OF nincomPOOPS AnD RICE PuDDInG STIRRERS. SO THERE."

He snarled and stuck out his slimy purple tongue.

"Prove it!" Sal's uncle said smugly and folded his arms. "Shoot a satellite out of the sky or something."

"EASY PEASY LEMON QUEASY!"

Sal looked at Freddy. Freddy looked at Sal's uncle. They all looked at Alan on the TV, who grinned. Then there was the slightest hint of a high-pitched whistle. Freddy looked up. The whistle was getting louder and louder.

Suddenly there was a huge

SMASH!!!

3 p.m.

"What on earth was that?" Freddy yelled, rushing to the window.

Sal, Freddy and Sergeant West ran out into the road. There, in the middle of the street, lay a steaming pile of solar panels and electric wires.

"Don't go near it!" Sergeant West warned.

"It's a satellite. It's only a blooming satellite," Freddy said, looking up.

"It could be a coincidence...?" Sergeant West said, taking off his hat and running his hands through his hair. Freddy looked at him and raised an eyebrow. He had a talent for raising an eyebrow but rarely got to do it, and this felt like the perfect situation for eyebrow raising. "Well it could be!" protested Sal's uncle.

"Whatever this is, it's from outer space," Sal said, pointing. "Look..."

On the side of the satellite was a big American flag and the words:

PROPERTY OF NASA.

IF FOUND CALL THIS

TOLL-FREE NUMBER:

021304531298754312

"Well at least we've got a phone number for them now." Freddy smiled, writing it down quickly.

"Quick! Inside before anything else lands on our heads," Sal said. All three hurtled back into the station. Sergeant West grabbed the TV.

"WHAT DID YOU DO THAT FOR?"

he screamed at the screen. There, calmly doing his nails – all three of them – was Alan.

"YOU SILLY NOGGIN mAn. YOU ASKED mE TO PROVE A PROOF TO YOU, SO I DID. nOW YOU ARE LAUGHING ON THE OTHER SIDE OF YOUR mAnY FACES. I nEED TO BE DOING THE nAPPING

46

BEFORE THE INVADING OTHERWISE I'LL BE GRUMPY. I WILL SOON HAVE THE RECIPE FOR THE PUDDING RICE WHEN I NIBBLE ON YOUR BRAINS."

And with that he was gone again.

"OH WELL FINE, WE WOULDN'T WANT YOU TO BE IN A BAD MOOD WHEN YOU KILL US ALL!"

Sal yelled sarcastically.

At that very second the office phone rang. Sergeant West picked it up. On the other end of the line was what sounded like a very angry man. "Yes I know Captain McGill, we heard the crash too. A satellite's gone down. How do I know?" Sergeant West looked at Freddy and Sal. "I think it's best if you sit down, Captain."

Five minutes later Captain Phil McGill was at the police station. He was a gruff-looking fellow, with thick arms and a neck that flopped over the collar of his tight shirt. He had tiny angry eyes and he smelt of coffee and dusty rooms.

"Now what's all this about an alien

invasion? Have you been on  the Stilton again, West?"

"No, it's true!" Sergeant West said, "I was sceptical too when my nephew and his mate burst in here, but then this creature appeared on TV and said he was going to shoot down a satellite. And then, well, he did."

"First things first, I don't believe in little green men; second of all, I don't care if it was Lady Gaga who shot the satellite down – I want this person arrested. It must have been a navigation satellite, because I have just seen a lorry carrying underpants spill its load onto the road. The imbecilic driver was clearly trying to fix his Sat-Nav rather than look where he was going. I had to swerve to avoid all the pants.

No one's going to want pants with my skid marks on are they?"

"BHAHAHA!" Sal laughed.

"OH, GROW UP!"

the Captain bellowed back.

"Sorry," Sal muttered.

"Right, now what are we going to do about this satellite?"

"Well, I have an idea," Freddy said. "Let's call NASA."

"Yes, hello, is that NASA? My name's Captain McGill. We've got one of your satellites lying here; an eye witness informs me that it's been shot down by an alien. You're putting me through to your supervisor? Yes, well I thought you might ... oh yes, hello. Yes that's what I said. Aliens, yes. Yes, we've made contact, well I haven't, a young man has. I'll pass you over."

Freddy held the phone to his ear. "I'm putting you on speaker-phone," the voice told Freddy. "Now tell them what the Captain just told me, kid."

"Hello, can you hear me?" Freddy asked nervously.

In a huge room, far away in America, the air hung heavy with heat. This was Mission Control, where they launched rockets. Real space rockets that actually went into space. The room was filled with technicians, astronomers and scientists of every kind. They were all listening silently. A man in spectacles took them off and wiped the sweat from his brow.

"We can hear you kid, go ahead. My name's Jim, I'm the director of NASA."

"Okay, well it all started when we were trying to watch the wrestling."

"Well it's Wrestlegeddon Smack Down, I don't blame you," Jim agreed.

"Yeah, well, we couldn't get the feed on our TV, so I hooked up a satellite thingy I'd made out of some tin foil and used a basic

TV output unit to double the strength of it. I guess pointing it at next door's satellite doubled the strength again, and because that one was pointing into space eventually all the satellites must have magnified the signal or something..."

"Meaning that the satellites all linked together to act like a giant antenna, shooting a signal into deep space..."

"Exactly!" Freddy said enthusiastically.

"Smart kid."

"Before I knew it, there he was. He calls himself Alan, from the planet Twang. He said they've been watching our TV signals as they drifted into space, but they didn't know where we were. It was only when I sent up a signal, unintentionally, that they found our planet. Alan said they want to take over our world and learn from us, but the only way to do that is by eating our brains."

"Oh my," Jim said.

"Yes, I know, I'm sorry. He says his planet is full of warriors and that there's only room for one planet like that in the universe. I think that's what they do, they fly from planet to planet killing everyone in their wake!" Freddy said, exasperated. "You have to believe me."

"Oh, I believe you kid. Whatever took down that satellite wasn't from earth. We also tracked some kind of spaceship from deep space. We didn't have time to hook onto it though; it's travelling too fast. Tell me Freddy, what's he like, the one called Alan? Is he intelligent?"

"Hmm, depends what you mean by intelligent," Freddy said, scratching his head. "He's sort of clever, in an annoying-little-brother sort of way. You know, if your little brother spoke weirdly and was obsessed with rice pudding. He said we've got until 10 p.m. tonight."

The words hung in the air for all to hear.

"I think we need to get the President involved. Will you hold the line, Freddy?" Jim asked.

4p.m.

Freddy looked at the others. There was silence, you could hear a pin drop … although technically no one can hear a pin drop; you can hear one land, but that's beside the point. What *is* the point is that it was very quiet.

Then the phone line crackled back into life. "The President's in a meeting in Paris, give me a moment," Jim said.

"SMILE!" Sal suddenly shouted,

pulling out his phone. "Extreme selfie time!"

"What are you doing?" Freddy barked.

"I was bored, what's happening?" Sal nudged Freddy in the ribs.

Freddy put his palm over the receiver.

"They've gone to get the President." he mouthed to the others.

"Oh..." said Sal. "The President of what?"

"OF AMERICA!"

Freddy, Sergeant West and Captain McGill yelled back.

"All right, all right – that's what I thought. I was just checking. You know, it might have been a different one. The American President lives in that house … oh, what's it called … you know, the really white one?"

"THE WHITE HOUSE!"

everyone shouted out once again.

"No need to yell, I'm feeling very got at. I've had a rough day, my head still hurts from being a human satellite dish and falling off that chair you know."

"What?!" Sal's uncle snapped.

"Err … nothing that's important,"

Freddy said, trying to change the subject. "Shouldn't we be doing something? They're calling the President. Shouldn't we get in touch with, I dunno, the authorities or the prime minister, someone who's got the power and menace to stop this sort of thing?"

"You mean, Hilda the lollipop lady?" Sergeant West piped up.

"Or like a General in the army or something?" Freddy suggested.

"I'll make a call," the Captain said.

"I still think Hilda would be better," Sal's uncle sniffed.

"Freddy, you still there?" came Jim's voice from down the phone.

"Yes, YES, I'm here."

"I've got the President on the line. You ready?"

"Yes, I'm ready." Freddy gulped.

There was a pause, a crackle, then a booming voice came down the phone line. "FREDDY, IS THIS RIGHT, AM I TALKING TO FREDDY?"

"Yes, Madam President. Do I call you Madame President? It does seem a bit weird, I mean you're not French, are you? I know you're in France, but that doesn't make you French, but Lady President sounds weird, as does Mrs President. You know what, I should probably shut up and let you talk, I'm just a little nervous and babbling, and yet here I am still talking, it's like I can't stop, please someone stop me!" Freddy said desperately.

"It's okay Freddy," the President responded. "You can call me Frances if you like, it doesn't matter. What I'd like to say first of all, is that you've been very brave and from what I hear, very clever too. You are the first ever human to make contact with another life form. We now have the answer to the question that has troubled mankind since the dawn of time ... are we alone? I just wish it was under better circumstances, that's all. It looks like these individuals are not friendly. They intend to do us harm. Freddy, here's what I need you to do. I want you to go home, wait for—" there was a

pause as Freddy heard the President ask Jim something— "seriously, he's called Alan? Okay, Freddy I want you to go home and wait for this Alan to contact you again."

"Yes, Lady President, Madam Frances, President, Sir … woman. Yes." Freddy's head slumped into his shoulders in embarrassment.

"Thank you, Freddy," the President chuckled. "I had no idea I had so many names. I need to ask one more thing of you before you go. This is very important. Please do not tell anyone about this. The last thing we want to do is spread panic. So keep the news to yourself and those who are in the room. We will be at your house as soon as we can."

"Yes, Mrs President. Goodbye." Freddy hung up the phone. "Brilliant, now she thinks I'm an idiot," he said, shaking his head.

"Nonsense, you're the person who discovered aliens. You'll go down in history!" Sal looked at his watch. "Well, for the next six hours, until every human

on earth gets their brains eaten, but you know, beggars can't be choosers – send!"

There was a

sound as Sal pressed his thumb on the phone.

"Right, here's what we have to do," Freddy began. "We have to go back to mine and wait for Alan to make contact again. The President—"

"Is that Mrs Madam Lady Frances President Woman?" Sergeant West chuckled.

"Yeah, okay, okay! The President said – and this is very important—" suddenly, Freddy stopped talking. He turned slowly to Sal. "What did you just say?" Freddy asked, his eyes narrowing. "You said 'send'. There was a whoosh sound."

"Oh, yeah, that was just an extreme selfie I posted online. Got to keep the followers happy." Sal smiled.

"What, what did he say?" Captain McGill barked, looking confused. "None of those words made any sense to me!"

"Please tell me you didn't tell anyone about this?" Freddy asked, panic in his eyes. Sal handed Freddy the phone. Freddy read out what Sal had written.

> We've just discovered life on another planet!
> **#extremeselfie #aliensfromoutofspace**
> **#theendoftheworld #Wolverhampton**
> **#Freddyshouse #eatmybigbrain...**

Freddy put his head in his hands. "She just told me not to tell anyone!"

"WHAT THE RUDDY NORA IS A HASHTAG? WHY IS NO ONE SPEAKING ENGLISH ANY MORE?" the captain bellowed.

"I'll delete it!" Sal said, grabbing the phone. "Oh dear..."

"WHAT ... WHAT?!"

Freddy cried.

"Out of battery."

"We'll have to sort it out later. We need to get back to mine – the President is on her way."

"It'll be fine." Sal said. "I've only got three followers: my nan, my cousin in Manchester and the local takeaway."

"What? The cousin that's been on TV, the famous one?" Freddy asked, looking worried.

"Oh, oops..." Sal laughed nervously.

Freddy, Sal, Sergeant West and Captain McGill dashed out of the police station and squeezed past the still-smoking satellite that lay on the road. Just at that second a truck crashed into a tree on the other side of the road.

"Sergeant West, get on the radio and put out a message to tell people to stop trying to fix their Sat-Navs and start looking where they're going. Someone's going to get killed!" McGill snapped.

"Yes Captain!" Sergeant West replied, grabbing his radio.

"LOOK, THE TRUCK!" Sal shouted. "IT WAS CARRYING DOUGHNUTS."

Everyone turned round. Sure enough, there were doughnuts lying all over the floor.

"The driver's fine," Freddy added, as he watched the driver get out of the cab, looking rather annoyed that he'd just ruined his delivery.

"Doughnuts ... my favourite, just lying there," Sal said.

"Sal, we have to go, we have orders from the President," Freddy said, looking at his watch.

Just then, an ice cream van came round the corner and bashed into the doughnut truck. There were now warm doughnuts and ice cream everywhere.

Sal whimpered. "Ice cream toooooo! Literally all my favourites."

"Sal, we have to go! We don't have time for doughnuts and ice cream!" Freddy cried.

Just then a lorry full of spoons came careering into the back of both trucks.

"OH COME ON!"

Sal yelled. Captain McGill grabbed Sal and ushered him down the road towards Freddy's place.

"But the doughnuts…"

"But the end of the world!" McGill yelled back.

"This is so confusing. I want to save the world, but I don't think you know how much I really like doughnuts and ice cream," Sal kept whining as he was dragged round the corner and the doughnuts and ice cream disappeared from view.

Back at the house, after avoiding the many crashed cars that were littered along the way, Freddy found his keys and opened the door. All of them dashed upstairs to his room and burst in.

"Right!" Freddy yelled, taking control of the situation. "Nobody touch the satellite dish—"

Sal coughed.

"Okay ... nobody touch the cone covered in tin foil that the dog had when he had his bits done. That's how we picked up the signal. If we move it, we might not hear from Alan again. Sergeant West, could you be in charge of making sure no one touches it? Who knows when they'll get in contact again. Perhaps Alan's already tried."

"There's only one way to find out!" Sal yelled, heading over to the fish bowl.

"NO, SAL, PLEASE NO!" Freddy called out.

"Perkins, has anyone from another planet been in touch on the magic light box we call the TV?" Sal said, puffing out his cheeks like a fish and getting as close to the bowl as he possibly could without getting in and having a swim.

"West, what's the matter with your nephew? He appears to be talking to a fish."

"It's okay, Captain, he just thinks this fish can talk that's all," Freddy tried to explain.

Sergeant West just looked embarrassed and shrugged his shoulders. "Kids, they can be so creative!" he chuckled.

"That's not creative, that's just weird, West," Captain McGill barked in his no-nonsense way. "You have a weird nephew, West."

"So creative..." Sergeant West muttered under his breath, ignoring the Captain.

"Everyone, we're getting distracted," Freddy said. "Sal, once again. Fish. Cannot. Talk. Can we stay focused? We only have a few hours to save the planet. We need to work as a team."

"He's right," Captain McGill agreed.

Just then, the room began to shake. Books shifted on their shelves and the light fitting rattled. There was a distant roar that began to build.

"This is it; this is the end of the world!" Sal put his hands over his ears. Everyone fell to their knees as dust from the wall cascaded down. Freddy grimaced and looked at his watch again.

"WAIT, IT'S TOO EARLY!" he yelled, but no one could hear him. Suddenly, Freddy recognized the sound.

It wasn't the end of the world at all. He struggled up and looked out of the window. He smiled with relief. "It's all right," he said to the others, "it's just a helicopter!"

But his jaw dropped as he looked out onto the front lawn at the huge green and white helicopter, which said in bold letters:

PRESIDENT OF THE UNITED STATES OF AMERICA

The doors of the helicopter swung open, then a couple of burly men in dark glasses jumped out. They took a quick look around before a small woman

headed out. They all ran towards the front door.

"The President's here – that was her helicopter!" Freddy shouted. Slowly but surely everyone got to their feet and dusted themselves off.

"I wasn't scared..." Sal said, wiping his brow.

"I WAS. I NEARLY FILLED MY PANTS!" Captain McGill yelled. "That cheese and onion pasty I had for lunch nearly shot out of my bottom. Open a window Sal."

"WHAT?" Sergeant West shouted back, hitting his head to stop the ringing in his ears. "Who's been shot in the bottom?"

Freddy galloped down the steps, but just before he opened the door, he took a deep breath. "Madam President, thank you for coming so quickly," he said calmly, managing to say her name without adding any unnecessary words into the mix.

"NO PROBLEM FREDDY!"

she shouted in a loud-no-nonsense-American-sort-of-way, but in a nice-loud-no-nonsense-American way if you see what I mean. "Sorry about your lawn. And sorry we're late; the Sat-Nav was down so we went a bit wrong," the President said, glaring at her security guard, who looked suitably embarrassed.

"Oh no worries, I'm sure Mum and Dad won't mind about the lawn," Freddy said, trying to work out how on earth he was going to explain to his parents why a helicopter was parked in their garden. "Come upstairs."

Immediately, the two security guards ran up the stairs to make sure it was safe, before the President hurried after them.

"Oh, by the way," she yelled, "meet the French President and his translator. We were in a meeting; it was quicker to bring them along than explain what was happening."

"Cripes, pleased to meet you. Bonjour!" Freddy said, completely exhausting all the French he knew in one fell swoop.

"Hello!" the French President smiled back, completely exhausting all the English he knew too, before saying something in the translator's ear.

"The President is very much liking to meet you and hopes that we can be stopping the world from exploding very soon."

"Did this guy and Alan have the same English teacher?" Freddy whispered under his breath.

"My name is the Marc, I am a translating today. Today is also my first day as doing the translator. Is it always this exciting, little Freddy?"

"Not sure – this is my first day discovering aliens from outer space. Shall we go on up?"

Freddy bolted upstairs to his bedroom. It was quite a bizarre sight. There were two security guards by the windows, keeping a careful eye on the American President, who was doing an extreme selfie with Sal. Sergeant West was smacking his truncheon into his hand, guarding a cone with tin foil on it, and Captain McGill was wafting his trousers. The French President said something to his translator.

"The President can smell a whiff," Marc announced.

"Oh, yes well..." McGill began to blush.

"It is a fine cheese or something; we had no idea you were a connoisseur of the cheeses. What is it?" Marc asked politely.

"Anyone know the French for 'semi-digested cheese and onion pasty'?" Captain McGill asked.

"I think I'll open a window," Freddy laughed awkwardly, "and let the whiff waft out of here."

"Let the riff-raff out?" Sergeant West

piped up, still trying to shake the ringing from his ears. "Right you are son, get out you horrible lot!" he began, swinging his truncheon at the American President. "Enough's enough!"

The two guards pulled out their guns and pointed them at Sal's uncle. "Put your baseball bat down Sir or I'll blow you to kingdom come!" one yelled. It's hard to

know which one as they both looked the same – let's pretend he's called Julian.

"Aargh!" Sal cried. "Don't shoot my uncle!"

"That's not a baseball bat, how dare you!" A wild West yelled.

"NO! STOP! SERGEANT WEST, NOT LET THE RIFF-RAFF OUT, LET THE WHIFF WAFT OUT. NO ONE'S GOING ANYWHERE. NO ONE'S GOING TO EAT ANY CHEESE. CAN WE ALL JUST STOP AND CALM DOWN AND GET ON WITH THE MATTER IN HAND?!"

Freddy screamed, getting to the very end of his tether.

"Stand down!" the American President agreed. "Always with the 'kingdom come!' Enough already."

"Okay, calm down, no need to shout everyone," Sal said.

"No one is shouting," Freddy said, trying to calm down.

"FREDDDDY!"

came a shout from downstairs. Freddy gulped. There was a thundering up the stairs. The door opened. There, with their hair full of twigs, leaves falling off their clothes and each clutching two

bags of tulip bulbs, were Freddy's mum
and dad.

"WHY IS THERE A HELICOPTER
PARKED ON MY LAWN?" Mum
bellowed before scanning the room.
"Who are these people and what, for the
love of all that is human, is that smell?"

Freddy took a deep breath and, speaking in his fastest voice ever, said, "The lady over there is the President of America, she's come to help save the world from an evil alien race that I sort of discovered while trying to watch the wrestling this afternoon with Sal. Oh, and it's cheese and onion pasty farts."

"WHAT!" Freddy's dad yelled. "YOU'VE BEEN TRYING TO WATCH THE WRESTLING AGAIN?!"

"Bigger picture, Dad, bigger picture."

"Oh yeah, right. Sorry. Wait, did you say aliens?"

"Yep."

"That would explain the crowds in the

street and possibly that TV crew wanting to know about the end of the world."

"What did you say to them?" Freddy asked his dad.

"I said that the spring had been particularly wet, but if we put the tulip bulbs in now, then we should see a decent bloom, certainly not the best, but not the end of the world either. I wondered why he looked at me funny."

"Sal," Freddy said, "did you delete that selfie?"

"Oooo, no, not yet – I mean I'm on it. GOOD GRIEF!" Sal yelled. "Okay, it seems that I've now got a few more followers," he said, plugging his phone in.

"Oh no, how many times has it been posted?" Freddy sighed.

"More than three, fewer than twelve million," Sal chuckled, slightly proud of himself.

"Don't worry, it was bound to get out some time," said President Jones. "We have more important things to worry about now."

"YES THAT IS RIGHT YOU VERY mUCH DO HAVE, LIKE WHEn I TAKE OVER THE WORLD, THE HOmE YOU CALL PLACE. SOON HUmAns, YOU WILL BE DOING THE DYING AnD I WILL BE KiNG OF YOUR BLUE SOGGY BALL OF PLANET. WHAT DO YOU THinK OF mE nOW YOU STiNKY EARTH APES?"

Everyone turned around, and there, on the screen, was Alan. His nap was meant to calm him down but he was awake and angrier than ever.

"Wow," said Marc, "his speaking the English is the very good."

The room was silent. Everyone stared open-mouthed at the TV.

"Alan – is it Alan? Can I call you that? My name is Frances Jones, I am President of the United States of America. Can I say first of all how good it is to meet you. I hope that we can be friends. We have so much to learn from each other."

Just at that second, the door to Freddy's room flung open again, and dozens of men and women fell in, speaking every language you could think of. Some of them looked like President Jones' security guards. Freddy wondered if there  was a place where they all shopped – a place that only sold black suits and sunglasses. The rest – from what Freddy could make out – were world leaders and probably translators.

A bald-headed man with steely blue eyes pushed his way to the front.

"Aha! I knew it. You were trying to claim all the glory yourself!" he said in a thick Russian accent.

"Oh Vladimir," President Jones sighed.

"It wasn't like that."

"We were supposed to be having a meeting when suddenly you and the French President dashed off in a helicopter. Don't you think that you should have told the rest of us? You left us looking like nitwits. We should all have been here to see the alien man for ourselves."

"WHO IS THIS mAn WITHOUT THE
HAIR On HIS HEAD? I DOn'T LIKE HIm,
HE'S TOO SHIny In mY EYEBALLS."

Alan said, covering his face.

"This is the Russian President," President Jones replied before turning to the man. "How did you find us?"

Vladimir pulled out his phone. "Some guy called Sal tweeted it. #Freddyshouse."

"Hashtag, hell yeah!" Sal yelped.

"Well never mind, you're here now," President Jones huffed.

"DON'T FORGET US!"

came several voices from the back of the crowd.

"Okay, okay. Alan, the Russian, French, Italian, Chinese and German leaders are here too, as well as—" President Jones strained her neck— "the Spanish, Brazilian, Japanese, Nigerian and British prime minister."

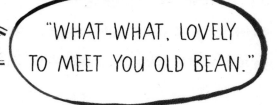

"WHAT-WHAT, LOVELY TO MEET YOU OLD BEAN."

came the faint greeting from the back of the room.

"WHO'S FOR TEA AND A MUFFIN?"

"Anyway, I think it's fair to say we are all delighted to meet you and that all we want is peace," President Jones said, smiling at Alan as if he were an angry toddler in danger of having a tantrum – a hungry angry toddler that is. The worst sort.

"HA, YOU mAKE mE TO Do THE LAUGHING OUT LOUD AGAIN, YOU HumAnOIDs ARE SILLY IN THE WORDs THAT YOU SPOUT OUT."

"I can assure you that we mean it, Alan. We can learn from each other, and I don't mean by eating our brains. Please – and I can't emphasize this enough – please don't eat our brains," President Jones asked firmly.

"I WILL DO AS I PLEASE, FOR I AM THE FEARSOME WARRIOR CALLED ALAN! WE HAVE BEEN DOING THE WATCHING OF YOUR PLANET FOR THE MANY YEARS, SEEING HOW YOU BEHAVE FROM THE TELEVISUAL SIGNAL THAT YOU HAVE BEEN PINGING INTO THE STARS. YOU DON'T WANT THE PEACE AND CUDDLES, YOU LIKE TO FIGHT AND ARGUE ALL THE TIME. YOU ARE ANGRY HUMANOIDS AND YOU NEED TO BE DISAPPEARED."

"That's not true. Take it back or I'll give you a knuckle sandwich!" Vladimir growled at Alan before ripping off his shirt.

"Really?" the Italian prime minister hollered. "That's the fourth time today!"

"Oops, sorry everyone," Vladimir said.

"I can assure you we are a peaceful race. Yes, we have arguments sometimes," President Jones said, glancing at the Russian President, "but we know that the best way to solve things is to talk,

to share, to help each other. Surely it is better to be friends than enemies? Besides, I don't understand, if you think we're terrible people, why do you want to learn from us?"

"FIRSTLY, BRAINS DO TASTE VERY DELICIOUS IN OUR BELLIES; SECONDLY, WE WANT TO LEARN THE SECRET OF THE MAGICAL SOUP YOU CALL RICE PUDDING; AND LASTLY, WE LOVE THE HUMOROUS FUNNY PEOPLE CALLED THE 'CHUCKLE BROTHERS', AND WE WANT TO LEARN THEIR WAYS. THE UNIVERSE WILL BE BETTER OFF WITHOUT YOU. YOU ARE NAUGHTY SPACE ALIENS, ALWAYS SHOUTING AND GETTING ANGRY. YOU POISON THE AIR AND MAKE THE WATERS DIRTY. I'VE SEEN HOW YOU BEHAVE. THERE IS NO TURNING BACK NOW. WE WILL SEE YOU SOON."

The picture began to fade out, as if he was going through a tunnel.

"WE ARE PASSING JUPITER, mY SIGnAL IS VERY mUCH GETTInG WORSE. THIS IS THE LAST TImE ALAn GOES PAY-AS-YOU-GO ... I SHALL SEE YOU SOON, THEn IT WILL BE DEATH O'CLOCK!"

"Is there any way we can stop them?" President Jones asked the Russian President. Freddy looked at the two of them.

"You mean with missiles or something don't you?" Freddy sighed sadly. "Isn't more violence bad?"

"More violence is bad, but we don't have much choice. We have to save ourselves. We have to do what we can

to stop this invasion. No one wants violence but sometimes, when the chips are down, when someone flies from the other side of the universe to slurp on one's brains, you have to fight back," the President said.

"You make a valid point," Freddy nodded.

"It's no good, Madam President," Vladimir wailed after speaking to one of his aides, "they're too far away, no missile can get them, even when they get into our atmosphere, they'll be moving too fast. Any missile that we fire will just miss and fall on us. We'll cause more damage than good."

"He's right," one of the security guards said, handing her a phone. Her eyes scanned it quickly.

"It's from NASA, they say the same thing. We're helpless."

7 P.M.

"You join us live outside a local supermarket. This place was just a quiet ordinary shop only a few hours ago; now it's on fire, all the windows are smashed and its produce has been stolen. It's happening right now in front of my eyes. In fact, I may be able to get an interview with one of the looters. Sir, Sir … what's your name?" The news reporter shoved his microphone into the face of an oncoming plunderer, whose arms were spilling over with all sorts of ill-gotten gains. All around him people were stealing what they could from the supermarket.

"Yes, hello?" The looter smiled, struggling to hold the huge TV that he was carrying under his arm.

"What's your name?" the reporter yelled above the sound of sirens.

"Reverend Ponsonby-Smyth," the gent smiled again, straightening his dog collar and waving shyly into the camera.

"Why are you stealing that big TV?" the reporter yelled again.

"Well, I popped in for some milk and I overheard someone talking about the end of the world. That's when chaos

broke out and people started to steal
stuff. I tried to tell the police, but they
were too busy pinching sweets and
chocolate to listen, so I thought, if you
can't beat them, join them. I mean, some
frightful chap from far away wants to
eat my brain, so I thought live a little.
Get that dream TV I've always wanted.
I can watch the cricket on it! What are

they going to do, put me in prison? Tomorrow there'll be no prison!"

"There'll be no cricket either! The world's about to end!" the reporter shouted, a tad confused.

"Oh, good point … I should have bought one of those recorder thingies, that way if I'm busy being eaten I won't miss it."

"But you won't get a chance to see it if you're dead!" the reporter said, looking at the camera. "You do know what the end of the world means? It means that you won't be able to do anything once it's happened."

"Oh, you're right, I feel silly for stealing this 'ripen at home' avocado now," the Reverend sighed shamefully.

"Want to buy a TV? I'll throw in a free avocado?"

"Not really..." the reporter muttered. "Have they got any DVD players left?"

"Oh yes, loads at the back; in fact I think I'll join you. I need to go back in – I forgot to pick up some custard for the weekend, my mother's coming over."

"THERE ISN'T GOING TO BE A WEEKEND. YOU ARE LITERALLY THE WORST LOOTER IN THE HISTORY OF LOOTING!!!"

"Oh yes, of course!" the Reverend said, determined to remember it this time.

"Well it's been quite a day for this reporter," he said, turning back to the camera. "Humans have made contact with aliens and in about three hours all humans will be killed. It feels like the world's collapsing. If it's all right by you, I'm off to join the looters, bag myself a few freebies. With that, back to the studio ... if there still is a studio that is."

Freddy turned off the news, it was just too miserable. It was a scene being played out all over the world. Where people were friends, they were now enemies, shops and houses were on fire and the world seemed to ring with the sound of police sirens. It was like something from a movie – a bad movie.

"Rightio, who wanted the tea with milk, who wanted it with sugar, who wanted it with both?" Freddy's dad said, offering around tea to the various world leaders now holed up in Freddy's bedroom. "President Jones?"

"One second," she said, her eyes full of concentration, "does yours have a hat?"

Vladimir stroked his chin, squinted at his card and, with a sigh of resignation, replied, "Yes."

"I knew it, it's Bernard!" the President yelled triumphantly, before turning around to Freddy's dad. "Thank you for the tea. I am, as I believe you say, parched! Do you have any of your English cookies, the ones that are pink and wafery?"

"Pink wafers? Yep I'll see what I can

do," Freddy's dad said, handing out the last of the mugs.

"I HATE THIS GAME. I'VE LOST EIGHT TIMES IN A ROW!"

Vladimir screamed, before ripping off his shirt again.

"Oh Vlad, put it away, no one wants to see," President Jones said, not even looking up.

"No wonder Alan thinks this planet is good for nothing except destruction. The world may be about to end and all we can do is fight and try to get one over on each other. I mean just look! People can't even have a game of Guess Who without it ending in semi-naked violence!" Freddy shouted. "Look at yourselves! What is the answer?"

"KerPlunk?" Vladimir suggested.

"Maybe Alan's right, maybe the universe is better off without us. We get angry at him because he wants to destroy us, but even if he left us alone, we're more than capable of destroying ourselves," Freddy sighed.

"The boy is right," the President of Russia agreed sagely as he velcroed up his shirt.

"Wait, does your shirt have Velcro instead of buttons? Have you just been velcroing your shirt up?" Sal asked.

"Yes, it was costing me a fortune every time I ripped it off; buttons aren't cheap you know. So I had a bunch of them especially made up with Velcro ... why are you all staring at me?"

"You know, and I say this as someone who talks to fish, you are the weirdest bloke I've ever met," Sal said.

"Never mind that," President Jones interrupted. "Freddy's completely right."

"Well what do we do about it?" The British prime minister asked. "Shall I put the kettle on?"

"Oh that is the answer you give for everything, tea, tea and more TEA!" Marc, the French President's translator, said.

"I didn't see the President say anything to you ... you weren't even translating!" The British prime minister snapped back.

"Oh, go have a cup of tea!" the German Chancellor chipped in.

"And what's wrong with tea?" the Chinese President interrupted.

"Right, that's it!" Marc the French translator yelled back, "no more mister guy who is very nice, it's no shirt time!" he growled.

"PARDON?"

the actual French President yelled.

"BRING YOUR MATES AND BRING YOUR DINNER!"

the British prime minister cried back. "Let's do this, Queensbury Rules what-what!" Then he rolled up his sleeves and put on a preposterous boxing pose by trotting forwards and backwards like a horse.

"Can someone be holding the jacket please?" Marc said, taking it off carefully. "Now, does one actually need to the ripping off the shirt, or can I take it off normally like I do when I go to sleepy bedtime? It's just it was a present from my mother for my birthday last week."

"Oh, happy birthday," the prime minister smiled back.

"Oh, thank you," Marc replied.

"You need to rip it, it's a show of strength and defiance," Vladimir chipped in.

"AAAAAARRRGH!"

Marc suddenly yelled. The French President, thinking this was some British custom, joined in with the screaming. Marc, thinking that he needed to translate the French President, started screaming even louder. Before long the French President and Marc were trapped in what can only be described as a scream-off.

"EVERYONE JUST SHUT UP!!!!!"

Freddy yelled. "What on earth are you doing? Can we, for the last time, try to get on, and even more importantly, try to keep our clothes on?"

"My boy is right," Freddy's mum said in a quiet but firm tone. "I don't mind Freddy having mates over but I will not tolerate this level of nonsense. Now, either you behave or I'll have to call your mums and dads and ask them to come and collect you and there will be no more playtime for anyone."

"Sorry Freddy's mum," everyone replied in unison.

"Now, I believe this nice young lady was going to say something," Freddy's mum said, pointing at President Jones. "She's the only one playing nicely; you could all learn a lesson or two from her."

"Thank you, Freddy's mum. Now I think we all owe her a big thank you. She's given us tea and biscuits and brought out the games for us. So what do we all say?" President Jones said, egging everyone on with her eyes.

"Thank you," came the monotonous but grateful reply.

"So yes, as I was saying, perhaps the best thing we can do is be nice to each other. Maybe Alan will see it and leave us be, but more importantly, we need to be nice to each other because it's the right thing to do. Freddy, Sal, is there any way we can set up a webcam? I've got an idea."

Five minutes later, Freddy and Sal had a laptop rigged up – admittedly it was touch-and-go as to whether Freddy's mum could remember where she'd put the WiFi password, but once she'd tracked it down, they were good to go.

"Are we on? Can everyone hear me?" the President of America said, looking into the laptop camera. Sal gave her the

thumbs up. "Good. My fellow Americans, Brits, in fact my fellow humans, welcome and thank you for listening to me.

"I know there's a lot of scared people out there. I know the last few hours have been terrifying, and I know that the next few are going to be as well. But if this is to be our last few hours on this planet together, let's not fight and steal from each other, let's do what we humans do best. Show compassion for each other, love each other.

"Let's show the rest of the universe what we are: a brave people who achieve great things when we work together. So, stop stealing, stop rioting, stop doing wrong and start doing right for one last time. If this is the end, then let's go down

with dignity. It seems that our weapons can't stop them, all it would do is prolong the agony. I'm sorry, there is nothing more that can be done."

The world seemed to stop for a few moments, letting the President's words sink in. Slowly, and rather embarrassingly, things returned to normal. Fires were put out, shoplifting reverends returned their ill-gotten gains, and people started being nice to each other. Perhaps it's only when you're about to lose everything you have that you finally appreciate what you've got.

"Listen, West," Captain McGill started,

"I'm sorry for what I said about Sal. He's a good kid, and yes, he might think that fish can talk, but he isn't a bad lad." McGill went in to shake Sergeant West's hand, but he was having none of it and gave McGill a big hug instead.

"Thank you Captain. I've always looked up to you. You're the best boss I've ever had – I just want to squeeze you."

came a strange sound from McGill's not inconsiderable bottom.

"Now, you see what you've done now, West, is you've squeezed me so hard, a little bubble of gas has come out of my bottom."

"Should I let go?" Sergeant West asked, nervously.

"I think if you do, even more will escape. I need not remind you, this is a very small room and there are a lot of important people in here. Not to mention the fact..."

"It was a very big pasty?" Sergeant West asked.

"Exactly. I think we're better off staying like this; don't let go. Please don't let go of me West," McGill pleaded.

Over in the other corner of the room, Freddy and Sal looked on intensely.

"Is your uncle slow-dancing with the Captain?"

"I'm not sure. I hope not – for one thing, there's no music – but these are strange times, Freddy," Sal said. "Hey, I wonder who won the wrestling?"

"I completely forgot about that," Freddy chuckled to himself.

"Well, it's been a funny day," Sal sighed.

"You don't seem scared," Freddy said.

"I am, I mean, no one wants their brain to be eaten do they? Especially by someone called Alan. But you know,

I've had some good times on this planet, some real good laughs. We both have." Sal smiled at Freddy. "Nothing lasts for ever I guess, we just have to make sure that we have the best time in the short time we're around. Well, I've done that, because of you Freddy."

"Nah, it's because of you," Freddy replied, grinning.

President Jones wandered over to the window, pulled back the curtain and looked up at the sky. The light had already started to fade and the stars were beginning to twinkle.

"I used to think my street was the dullest place in the universe," Freddy said, gazing up at the stars.

"Well not any more; now it's the most famous street in the world," the President said, staring at it.

"Yeah, but not in a good way." Freddy puffed his cheeks out. "I mean, who wants to be remembered as the place that started an invasion of brain-eating aliens from outer space? I'd prefer 'best kept roundabout in England' if I'm honest."

"You're not responsible for this." The President patted him on the shoulder. "If it wasn't you, then it would have been someone else."

"I dunno, maybe if I'd said something different, we wouldn't be in this mess." Freddy shook his head.

"Rubbish!" Sal interrupted. "We didn't ask for this. No one's to blame for a bully's behaviour other than the bully."

"Sal's right," Vladimir agreed. "I realize I have been a bully too. I would like to say sorry and assure you that from now on, no matter how complicated things get, I promise to keep my clothes on."

"The world thanks you," Freddy smiled.

"Madam President, we've been tracking an object entering out solar system," one of the President's advisors told her. "It's moving too quickly to be a satellite – it must be them."

"Where is it?" Freddy asked.

"A few hundred miles away. It's heading straight for us. If you look out of the window, you should be able to see it any moment."

For a second, no one moved. Then the

rest of the room bolted to the window.

"I don't see anything," Sal's uncle said, his nose pressed against the glass.

"Look, there!" Freddy said, his eyes fixed above a fast food restaurant in the distance.

"Wow, it looks beautiful," Sergeant West said. "I could really go for a cheeseburger right now."

"No, not the burger place, above it!"

"Oh yeahhh..." they all muttered under their breath.

"I always fancied going into space," Freddy said to no one in particular.

"It's amazing," Vladimir said, smiling.

"You've been up there?" Sal asked, surprised.

"Yeah, years ago. Before I was the coolest President Russia ever had, I was a cosmonaut. I flew a rocket up there. We said it was a science mission, but it was really to check if America had actually made it to the moon like they said." Vlad gazed up at the stars, as if he was homesick for his previous life.

"And had they?" asked the Brazilian leader.

"Yeah, it was really annoying," the Russian President chuckled.

"What's it like?" President Jones asked him, as if they were two old friends meeting after a long time.

"Amazing. You feel little and insignificant, but in a good way. It makes you realize that we're not a collection of different people, but we're all one really. Sad thing is that when you land, you hear the noise, all the shouting, all the anger – it sort of sweeps you up again and you get sucked into your old way of life. And before you know it, you're ripping your clothes off at the drop of a hat. That's chilly work in Russia you know."

He paused, pointing at the sky. "Look!"

There, a tiny twinkle that looked like a shooting star sailed towards earth. It looked amazing, beautiful even. Except it was only coming for one thing: to destroy them all.

9 p.m.

"How long before they arrive?" President Jones asked.

"We estimate within the hour," Vladimir said, speaking on his phone to experts back in Russia.

"What should we do?" Freddy said.

"Shall I put the kettle on?" Freddy's mum suggested.

"Well, it's kind of you to give them something to wash down our brains with, but no Mum, I say probably don't make them tea."

"What about…?"

"No coffee either," Freddy snapped.

"Let's not get bogged down with tea and brains," the American President interrupted. "The fact is that we can't stay here. Even if this is the end, I'm not going to give up and let them eat—let them walk all over us. While there's still time we should go out there and say something; even if it does no good, we have to keep trying."

"She's right," Freddy agreed. "Come on everyone, let's go."

"Uh, nobody's going anywhere until this room's tidied up – there's games everywhere. I don't know who's been playing marbles, but it's a death-trap. Now, there's going to be no end of the world until we've tidied up!" Freddy's dad yelled.

"Ohhh..." everyone moaned.

"None of that 'oh Dad' nonsense, let's just get on with it. There'll be a prize for who tidies the quickest."

"Dad, we're not kids, we're not going to fall for that old trick, turning everything into a competition."

"Really?" Dad said, smiling. Freddy turned around.

"Bet I can put the robot away before you can tidy up the train set!" President Jones cried.

"Oh yeah, and what if you

don't?" Vladimir said, grinning.

"We'll give you Alaska back!" She chuckled.

"It's on, like Donkey Kong," Vladimir laughed.

"I take it back," Freddy muttered.

Not long later, everyone left Freddy's now-tidy room and headed downstairs to the front door.

"Well I never wanted Alaska anyway," Vladimir huffed.

"Before we go out," Freddy said, "I just want to say thank you. Thank you for doing what you could to try to stop this. I also wanted to say sorry. Sorry for all the trouble I've caused. I know, I know you've said it's not my fault, but it was me, I was the one who made contact. And although we're about to get our brains eaten, maybe if there's one thing we can take from this it's that we did all learn to get along. Nobody's perfect, we're all just human. Maybe today of all days that's something to celebrate."

"Nice one son," Freddy's dad said before patting him on the shoulder. Freddy took a deep breath again and opened the door.

There was a huge crowd of cameras and news reporters, the odd furious lollipop lady, as well as every television station in the world. Some were carrying banners telling the aliens to go home – well they were using ruder words than that, but as this is a children's story I couldn't possibly repeat them. There were even people dressed up as aliens to welcome them – clearly trying to get on their good side and hopefully avoid getting their brains eaten.

The noise was almost unbearable. Everyone had something to say, or rather shout. Reporters yelled, hurling questions like snowballs at the various presidents and prime ministers.

President Jones tried to quieten the crowds down. She grabbed a microphone and started to speak into it.

"I hope you can all hear me," she said. The crowds stopped cheering or shouting (frankly it was hard to tell the difference). "People of the world, over the past few hours we have seen the best of us and the worst of us. We have seen how much fight we have in us, we have also seen our kindness. This has been a very difficult day for us all, but it has taken a boy called Freddy to show us how to behave like grown-ups. He has shown us that despite our differences, we are the same, and while we have the capacity to hurt, we have far more kindness in us than maybe we realize. This may be the end, but I am proud of this planet

and everyone on it. While there is breath in my body, I will try to persuade our attackers to change their mind. I will not give up!"

Everyone went wild. It was a rallying cry that the whole world could get behind. Strangers hugged each other – it didn't matter who they were, what they

looked like – it was an outpouring of happiness.

It seemed as if earth and the funny wobbly people who walked upon it were invincible.

Suddenly, the noise died down as a bright light descended over the street. In the sky, the twinkle that Freddy and everyone else had seen from the window had turned into a mini ball of fire as the spacecraft entered the earth's atmosphere. It was impossible to tell how big it was, or how far away it was. The crowds started to step back, and even the ones proclaiming to love the new alien killers were now running away. All the street lights went out, then the house lights too.

"It must be to do with the electrical magnetism. It's created a power surge and blown all the fuses," Freddy muttered under his breath.

"WHAT'S GOING ON?"

McGill yelled out into the darkness.

"It's an electrical magnetic surge," Sal said knowingly. "It must have caused all the fuses to blow out."

"I take it all back, West, your nephew is a clever lad," McGill said, patting Sal's uncle on the back.

Just as the sky went black, there was a huge gust of wind – not from McGill this time, but from high above. Dust was whipped up into the air, and everyone covered their eyes and their mouths. It was like being in a sandstorm in the Sahara, only in Wolverhampton.

Then after a few seconds, there was silence again as the wind dropped. No one could see anything except a bright light shining down from the heavens. Freddy suddenly felt his hands being grabbed; he looked over, it was Mum and Dad. He squeezed back. His heart was beating like a drum. Was this it, was this the end?

10 P.M.

It was hard to get any
bearings; there was com-
plete and utter darkness apart
from a single beam of light
and the sound of what Freddy
presumed was the spaceship's
engines slowing down. The crowds
hit the floor. Everyone was screaming.
Even Vladimir looked scared and he

never looked frightened. The dust swirled again, and billowed through the houses. Freddy clung to his mum and dad as fiercely as they clung to him.

"I picked a helluva day to stop ripping my shirt off!" Vladimir howled.

After a few moments, everyone got to their knees, using hankies and whatever they could find to cover their faces. Slowly but surely the dust and noise began to settle. The spaceship had landed.

The President stepped forward, and at the top of her voice yelled towards it.

"ALAN. WE ON EARTH ARE A FRIENDLY LOT ... MOSTLY. IT'S NOT TOO LATE FOR US TO BE FRIENDS. PEACE IS BETTER THAN VIOLENCE. I KNOW YOU CRAVE OUR BRAINS, BUT MAYBE INSTEAD OF EATING THEM, YOU COULD USE THEM IN A

DIFFERENT WAY. WE COULD
SHARE THE KNOWLEDGE OF
OUR TWO WORLDS. WE HAVE
LOTS MORE NICE THINGS TO
EAT DOWN HERE ... CUSTARD
FOR INSTANCE!"

the President thought on her feet.

"I'M PRETTY SURE IT'S NICER
THAN BRAINS. ON BEHALF
OF ALL EARTH, WE URGE YOU
AS A PLANET TO CHOOSE THE
VEGETARIAN OPTION!"

"SILENCE EARTH LADY PERSON, THE ONE THEY CALL mADAm PRESIDEnT!"

Alan's voice boomed out of the spaceship.

"YOU BORING BAnTER IS mAKING mE TIRED IN THE HEAD. I Am HUNGRY AFTER my LONG JOURNEY FROm THE ACROSS THE GALAXY. ALL ALAn WAnT TO DO IS STRETCH HIS LEG PARTS, DO A BIG WEE AnD EAT SOmE DELICIOUS BRAINS THANK YOU PLEASE!"

There was a whooshing sound as the door of the spaceship opened. Freddy could smell smoke pouring out of the craft, then a figure emerged from the dazzling light. Freddy could see an enormous alien shadow and what looked like the outline of a laser gun.

"YES OH GREAT ALAN, EATER OF THE
BRAINS, RULER OF THE UNIVERSE, THE
WIND BENEATH MY WINGS."

"This is it!" Freddy winced in terror.

There was the sound of footsteps, Freddy closed his eyes, as did everyone; not one person could bear to watch, like they were trying not to catch a teacher's eye in case they got extra homework. Then, Alan began to speak again.

"I SHALL EAT THE ONE CALLED FREDDY FIRST.
NOW HAND OVER YOUR BRAIN.

 FEED ME!!!!"

Freddy gulped. This was it, it was all over.

He decided to face the enemy at last. If he was going to get his brains eaten, he wanted to at least look them in the eye. Freddy walked towards the dazzling light, shielding his face with his hands. After a few steps he put his hands down and opened his eye a crack.

Nothing. He couldn't see anyone.

Then he felt a tickle on his leg.

"Are you kidding me?" Freddy yelled out.

"ARE YOU ACTUALLY KIDDING ME?!"

Everyone slowly opened their eyes. There, in front of them, were Alan and Brian, the two faces that had brought terror to planet Earth. It was them all right, except there was something different about them. They were only two inches tall. The aliens from outer space were no bigger than an egg. Their spaceship, which had been hidden in the smoke, was no bigger than a shoe box.

"HAND OVER YOUR BRAINS,"

Alan demanded again. The laser gun wasn't a laser gun at all. It was a tiny megaphone.

No one said a word. They just stared at the tiny invaders and the giant shadows they'd cast.

"WHY ARE YOU NOT OBEYING ME WITH MY ORDERS? WHY ARE YOU NOT SCAREDY DOGS?

HAND OVER YOUR BRAINS!"

"Or what?!" Freddy laughed. "Are you going to kick me in the shin? Oh no, wait, you'd have to get a ladder for that!"

"ERR, ALAN, LORD OF ALL SPACEMEN, KING
OF THE CASTLE, THE BIG CHEESE OF THE
GALAXY ...I SUGGEST WE MAKE A HASTY
RETREAT. THESE HUMANS SEEM TO BE
BIGGER THAN WE WERE EXPECTING."

"NONSENSE, LOOK AT THEM, THEY ARE
TERRIFIED, SEE HOW THEIR STUPID
HUMAN MOUTHS WAGGLE IN **FEAR**!"

Alan yelled at Brian.

"THAT'S CALLED LAUGHING, SIRE."

Everyone was beginning to giggle with relief and the absurdity that tiny two-inch aliens had just tried to take over the world.

"Where are all your many armies?" Freddy asked, peering down at the tiny spacemen.

"THE REST OF THE INVADERS WILL BE HERE IN A mO. THERE WAS TOO mAnY OF THE INVADERS TO FIT In THE OnE SPACESHIP, SO WE DID BROUGHT THE SPARE OnE."

"Wait, your entire planet can fit into two flying saucers!" Freddy asked. "How many of you are there?"

"WELL, LET mE DOinG mATHEmATICS RIGHT nOW,"

Alan said, counting his green fingers.

"THERE'S mE, BRIAn, OBVIOUSLY, THEn THERE'S DAVE, JULIAn AnD TRISHA."

"FIVE! There's five of you?! How many planets have you invaded?"

"THIS IS OUR FIRST TIME,"

Alan said, looking at his feet.

"I KNEW THIS WAS A BAD IDEA,"

Brian muttered.

"DON'T GIVE ME THAT LOOK, BRIAN, IT'S NOT
MY FAULT, THEY LOOKED SMALLER ON TV.
ANYWAY, THINKING ABOUT IT, I'M NOT THAT
HUNGRY, I MIGHT GO HOME, JUST REMEMBERED
I GOT SOME CRUMPETS IN THE FREEZER, FROM
WHEN I DID A BIG SHOP THE OTHER WEEK,
I GO HOME NOW, TATTY BYE-BYE."

"Oh, you don't get away that easy! LET'S
BLOW THEM TO KINGDOM COME!"
Vladimir yelled, about to rip his shirt off,

before remembering his vow to be a nice boy. "Maybe not."

"Can't we keep them, Uncle? They're so cute!" Sal cried.

"No!" Sergeant West replied. "Remember who begged for a rabbit and who was left to clear up its poo and clean out its cage?

Your parents won't do that again. No aliens for you young man."

"What should we do?" President Jones wondered. "They need to be taught a lesson."

"I know!" said Freddy. "Leave us alone. If you ever come near us, we'll send our most fearsome warrior to *your* planet instead!"

"Who's that?" Alan asked, looking scared.

Freddy put his fingers in his mouth and let out a huge whistle.

"Alan, meet Hilda!" he yelled, and with that Hilda grabbed her lollipop and ran towards Alan and Brian.

"QUICK, START UP THE ENGINES AND SET
THE SAT-NAV TO HOME, BRIAN!"

Alan shouted, running back into the tiny
spaceship that was parked on the road.

"THE SAT-NAV'S NOT WORKING, SIR. REMEMBER,
WE ACCIDENTALLY CRASHED INTO THAT SATELLITE,"

Brian reminded Alan.

"SHHHH, THEY THOUGHT WE SHOT IT DOWN.
WHY DO YOU ALWAYS EMBARRASS ME?!"

Alan screamed after Brian as they both ran
back to the spaceship. There was a quick
burst of engine noise, before the spaceship
reversed and zipped away into the night

sky, honking its horn as it went.

"Well, what a funny day," Freddy said, shrugging his shoulders.

"Do you know what we should do to celebrate?" President Jones said.

"What?" Sal and Freddy asked at the same time.

"Watch Wrestlegeddon Smack Down!" she grinned. "I have access to any TV station in the world; one of the perks of the job – that and the helicopter that is."

"BOOOOOOM!"

the President of Russia yelled, ripping off his shirt in excitement. "Now you're talking!"

"Excellent," Freddy's mum said. "Shall I pop the kettle on?"

High above the drama, in Freddy's room, in a dark corner where no one was looking, a tiny voice piped up from within the fish bowl.

"Well, you don't see that every day do you? I fancy a banana."

Perkins tutted to himself, before swimming off.

☆ Draw the Grumpiest Alien ☆ in the Universe

1. Start with the body.

2. Add two arms and gloves on each hand.

3. Then add two legs, two teeny tiny shoes and the detail for Alan's stylish space outfit.

4. Draw Alan's bushy
   eyebrows and his chin.

5. Add three eyes, a
   mouth and two ears.

6. Then the nose.
   Et voilà!

Alan's Guide to English

Greeting and salutations to your face from my face. I am very pleasurably proud to do the meeting of you.

Translation: Hello.

I am very much looking forward to arriving at your silly spinny blue planet to do the invading and exterminating of your silly human bodies.

Translation: Hello, I'm going to kill you.

I am in the need to be dunked in water and do the relaxing on a bed made of rubber and air, tell me now where this place is or I'll blow your face off.

Translation: Where's the swimming pool?

I am very much moving uncontrollably to the hot sound.

Translation: I enjoy the work of Lionel Richie.

The meteorites and gases of this stinking solar system make hard the conquering of your silly-stupid rock. I hate it. I hate it. I hate it.

Translation: Terrible weather we're having.

Alan's Top Tips for
Invading Another Planet

★ A map.

★ Lunch (I recommend the delicious rice pudding food or maybe some human brains).

★ A flask of milky tea.

★ Something to do to pass the time – like a game of glhjdgdtsuvfjfnfbfkffbfjkdskdjjbkjndkjbfkjkbsudjh-vdjhjhvjdvhasj6666ndbdhgd, or as you humans call it 'Twister'.

★ Spare pants.

★ The ability to tear through space and time as we know it, so you can travel at the speed of light.

★ Change for parking.

Lumpy-Bumpy Brain Puddings

You will need:

- 150g white chocolate
- 100g crisped rice cereal
- Green food colouring
- Mini marshmallows or glacé cherries

Directions

1. Break up the chocolate into a heat-proof bowl*. Put the bowl over a simmering pan of water and stir the chocolate until melted.

2. Very carefully, take the bowl off the heat and allow to cool. Add one drop of green food colouring to the chocolate and stir.

3. Pour the crisped rice into a larger bowl and add the melted chocolate. Mix until the chocolate has covered the rice.

4. When the mixture has cooled slightly, use a table spoon or an ice cream scoop to scoop up some of the mix. Spoon each portion onto a tray lined with baking paper.

5. Use your fingers to mould the puddings into brain-like shapes and decorate with mini marshmallows and/or glacé cherries.

6. Put the tray in the fridge to allow the puddings to set.

7. Proudly give a brain pudding to an unsuspecting relative, or smash to bits and eat yourself!

Always ask an adult to supervise when using a hob.

TOM McLaughlin

My name's Tom, I'm the fella who wrote and illustrated the book (illustrated is just a posh way of saying I drew the pictures). I'm here to tell you a little bit about myself. I used to be a cartoonist for a newspaper, it was my job to draw cartoons of prime ministers and Presidents. After that I started writing and illustrating my own books. I like football, fizzy sour sweets, laughing lots, sausages, staring out of the window and writing books. I have a silly children, three wives and a lovely dog ... no hang on, I mean I have a silly dog, three children and a lovely wife.

Find out more at **www.tommclaughlin.co.uk**

www.walker.co.uk